Ozma
Waywa

Ozma and the Wayward Wand

by Polly Berends
illustrated by David Rose

Random House New York

Library of Congress Cataloging in Publication Data: Berends, Polly Berrien. Ozma and the wayward wand. SUMMARY: While Dorothy is visiting the magic land of Oz, the royal gardener's son borrows Princess Ozma's wand without permission and endangers the Emerald City with uncontrollable spells. 1. Children's stories, American. [1. Fantasy] I. Rose, David S., 1947– , ill. II. Title. PZ7.B4482Oz 1985 [Fic] 84-17972 ISBN: 0-394-87068-9 (trade); 0-394-97068-3 (lib. bdg.)

Manufactured in the United States of America 1 2 3 4 5 6 7 8 9 0

Contents

1

Strange Happenings in Kansas

High in the twilight over Kansas a slip of white paper floated. It drifted slowly downward, rocking back and forth until a gentle wind caught and carried it—a small boatless sail—first over one farm, then over another. It traveled almost purposefully, as if searching for something.

Far below a small girl was walking from barn to house with a little black dog beside her. She did not see the paper floating in the darkening sky. She did not see it circle and begin to float down. She was looking at her feet, watching the dust that puffed up around her brown leather shoes.

"Nothing exciting ever happens in humdrum Kansas," she said to herself. "Schoolwork and chores. Chores and schoolwork. Drat!"

"Bow-wow-wow-wow!" The little black dog suddenly tore across the farmyard barking wildly.

"Toto, what is it?" the girl called.

She watched him dash across the yard, looking up as if he were following something. Now she, too, saw the white paper sailing just ahead of Toto. Despite the shortness of his legs the little dog ran terribly fast, jumping up and down as he went. At last in one strong leap he succeeded in snatching the white sheet out of the air. He held his head high so the paper would not drag in the dust. Triumphantly he trotted to the girl, bringing his prize for her inspection.

It was a flier—a printed announcement of the kind often dropped from airplanes to advertise auctions, political candidates, medicine shows, soap powders, and cattle feed. Dorothy read it eagerly.

"Oh, Toto!" she cried. "Listen to this!

  " 'Up, Up, and Away.
   Balloon Rides.
See the Whole State of Kansas from the Air.
Ride in the Wonderful Hot Air Balloon.
  Only Fifty Cents a Ride.
Saturday, Four O'clock, at the Kansas State Fair.'

9

"We almost rode in a balloon once, you know—all the way from the Land of Oz. If only you hadn't gotten lost. I couldn't leave without *you,* so the balloon left without us. Oh, Toto, wouldn't it be wonderful to go up in a balloon?"

"Bedtime, Dorothy!" called a voice from the farmhouse. "Hurry along, now."

"Coming, Aunt Em," said Dorothy. Inside she placed the flier on the table by the door. "No sense asking Aunt Em and Uncle Henry about a balloon ride," she said. "They need me to help with the chores. 'Sides, we can't afford it."

As Dorothy stood at the kitchen sink, washing up for bed, she half heard her aunt and uncle talking in low voices.

"Seems a might peaked," Uncle Henry was saying.

"Yep," said Aunt Em. "A bit long in the face, too."

"Might perk her up," said Uncle Henry.

Behind the curtain that separated Dorothy's bed from the rest of the one-room farmhouse,

Dorothy found her bedcovers turned back, as usual. As she and Toto jumped onto the mattress, up from the pillow bounced a shiny fifty-cent piece!

"Oh, Aunt Em! Uncle Henry! Thank you!" Dorothy cried, running out to where they sat.

There on the arm of Uncle Henry's chair lay the flier. Aunt Em rocked, darning socks as always. They didn't even look up as Dorothy bounded over.

"Nonsense, child," said Aunt Em. "Calm yourself, now."

"Off to bed," said Uncle Henry. "Have to be up mighty early if you want to get your chores done in time for the fair."

Dorothy kissed them both soundly before she went back to bed. She lay there a long time, thinking about Aunt Em and Uncle Henry, and about the balloon ride. Outside peepers and bullfrogs sang. It was a lovely, gentle song—a lullaby for sleeping and for dreaming. "Baalloon," sang one big bullfrog to another. "Baalloon," came the reply.

★   ★   ★

Dorothy's head turned back and forth as she and Toto walked through the fair. There was so much to see. Everywhere she looked she saw children on rides, children eating cotton candy and peanuts, and children running from one booth to another. But Dorothy did not join in. She was saving her money for the balloon ride. She patted her apron pocket. Yes, the fifty-cent piece was still there.

"Oops! Sorry!" A little boy bumped into Dorothy. He was carrying a huge stuffed lion, a prize from the ringtoss booth, and couldn't

see where he was going. The lion was bright pink. But just the same it reminded Dorothy of her old friend the Cowardly Lion.

Dear, sweet Cowardly Lion, she thought. *I wonder how he is.*

Suddenly she stopped. Before her stood a wooden crate on a pedestal. On the crate hung a big blue ribbon. 1ST PRIZE FOR YELLOWEST HEN, it said.

"That's odd, isn't it, Toto?" exclaimed Dorothy. "There aren't any yellow hens in Kansas!"

The only yellow hen Dorothy had ever seen was in Oz. How she would love to see her beloved Billina again! Dorothy peered through the slats of the crate. She couldn't believe her eyes!

"Is it really *you*, Billina?" she gasped.

But the yellow hen just blinked her eyes stupidly.

"Ca-daw-cut," the hen clucked, and turned away from Dorothy rudely.

"That is definitely *not* Billina," said Dorothy crossly. "Billina can talk. And she is *never* impolite."

"Let me tell your fortune, dearie," said a voice behind Dorothy.

Dorothy spun around so fast that she almost stepped on poor Toto. Peering out of a tent was a large woman with a turban on her head and many long strings of beads around her neck. The sign over the opening of the tent said MADAME ZSA ZSA. GYPSY FORTUNE TELLER.

Dorothy was surprised that Toto did not bark at Madame Zsa Zsa. Instead he stepped forward, wagging his tail in an almost familiar way. The woman beckoned Dorothy inside.

"Oh, no, thank you," said Dorothy. "I only have fifty cents, and I'm saving it for a ride in the hot air balloon."

Now Dorothy noticed something strange about the gypsy fortune teller's eyes. One was very different from the other. The look in the right eye was distinctly kind. The left eye was stern—not in a mean way, but in a definite, no-nonsense way. It was almost like looking at two different people.

Dorothy found herself unable to leave. The stern eye seemed to tell her that she dared not say no. The kind eye seemed to say she had nothing to fear. Hugging Toto close, Dorothy stepped into the tent and placed her precious fifty-cent piece in the woman's palm.

Inside the tent Madame Zsa Zsa towered over Dorothy and Toto. It was a very small tent, so there was only a tiny space left for them. Because the tent was green, the light that filtered through was also green. This made everything inside look emerald green as well. Even Madame Zsa Zsa. Even her crystal ball.

Dorothy peered into the crystal ball. Three small figures floated in its greenish light. One seemed to be a chicken. Another was a tall floppy fellow with a pointed hat. The third was a beautiful girl with a magic wand and a crown.

"Why, that's Billina—and the Scarecrow!" cried Dorothy. "And there is Ozma! Oh, how beautiful she is! And look, Toto, there is the Emerald Palace! Oh, Toto, we must go back to Oz soon! What a wonderful magical world it is!"

Madame Zsa Zsa held her crystal ball close to Dorothy's ear. Inside, Dorothy heard a small voice sigh. "I wish Dorothy would come back to Oz!" said someone who sounded just like Ozma. "Has she forgotten us?"

"No!" cried Dorothy. "I haven't forgotten you. It's just so busy here. But I want to come—and I will come soon! I promise!"

"Our time is up," said Madame Zsa Zsa, withdrawing the crystal ball.

Dorothy cast a last look at the crystal ball. The image of the Emerald Palace was gone. Now there were five figures inside where a moment ago there had been only three! Wait. No! They were not figures. They were fish—just plain old goldfish swimming around in the greenish-looking water.

"Why, that's not a crystal ball!" said Dorothy. "It's only a fishbowl. And those aren't my friends from Oz. They're nothing but fish! You tricked me!"

"There is a time for magic and a time for common sense," said Madame Zsa Zsa. "It is important to know which is which. For fifty cents that is all I can tell you."

Dorothy knew it was no use arguing with Madame Zsa Zsa, but she left the tent feeling unhappy. When she looked up and saw the wonderful balloon, she felt even worse. It would soon land at the fair. And it would soon go up without Dorothy.

"Oh, Toto," she said. "Why did I spend my money on that horrible fortune teller?"

The little dog licked Dorothy's hand comfortingly. Then Dorothy had a wonderful idea.

"We *will* go on a trip after all, Toto!" she said. "This very day. We shall return to the Land of Oz!"

When Dorothy had last left the Land of Oz, she and Ozma, the princess of the land, had made a special arrangement. Every Saturday morning, Ozma would look for Dorothy in her magic picture. Then, if Dorothy wanted to return to Oz, she had only to give a secret signal and she would be brought to Oz by magic. It was twenty minutes before twelve o'clock! If she and Toto hurried, they would get home just in time to signal the princess.

But just then the crowd caught sight of the balloon.

"Here it comes!" someone shouted. At once everyone began running. Hundreds of people leaned, shoved, and jostled each other forward, pushing Dorothy and Toto along with them. Soon Dorothy's feet no longer touched the ground, and before long she had been carried to the very front of the crowd. Thus, quite against her own wishes, she was the very first one in line for the balloon.

"Step right up, young lady," said the balloon man.

The huge orange-and-blue-striped balloon towered above Dorothy. How she would love to go up in it! But right now she wasn't going anywhere! She could not get home in time for the magic picture, and she could not ride in the balloon either.

"I can't, sir," she said sadly. "I have no money to pay."

"Nonsense," said the balloon man. "First

come, first served. You are the first in line, so you shall be the first to go up—money or no money."

"Oh, thank you, sir!" said Dorothy, amazed.

Strong arms lifted her into the passenger basket of the balloon. Then the balloon man himself climbed aboard. He untied the balloon from its mooring and released a few bags of sand from the edge of the passenger basket. Then he turned up the little gas fire that filled the balloon with hot air. The balloon shook as it strained to take off. Then over the sound of the fire the two passengers heard a dog barking and yelping desperately.

"It's Toto!" cried Dorothy, peering over the edge of the basket. "That's my dog, Toto! We can't leave poor Toto behind! He'll get lost. Oh, please, mister. Please get my dog!"

In a split second the balloon man had jumped out of the basket and scooped up Toto. But he had not reckoned on the effect of the loss of his weight. By the time he turned to hand Toto to Dorothy, the lightened balloon was already airborne. He threw Toto up to

Dorothy and tried to leap up himself, but he only succeeded in grabbing on to the basket with one hand. He struggled to climb aboard, but it was no use. At fifteen feet he had no choice but to let go and drop back down to the ground. There was a sigh and a groan from the crowd as the balloon surged upward.

"Oh, dear," said Dorothy. "I'm sorry. I didn't mean to cause so much trouble. It was so nice of you to let me—"

Then she stopped, for she suddenly realized that she was much too high up to be heard.

As the balloon rose the crowd grew smaller. Then the fair grew small as well. For a time Dorothy could even see Aunt Em and Uncle Henry's farm, but soon she was even too high for that. Higher and higher the balloon rose until, as the flier had promised, they could see all of Kansas. Higher and higher they went until the whole state of Kansas was as small as a postage stamp.

As often happens in Kansas, and as had happened to Dorothy several times before, a tremendous wind suddenly blew up from nowhere. The balloon began to travel very fast, over the land and far away. Dorothy looked down. Was she really being blown away? Or was it the postage stamp of Kansas that the wind was carrying off? And was this the same wind that just yesterday had brought the flier to Dorothy? Dorothy was quite certain that the answer was yes.

As unexpectedly as it had blown up, the wind died down. Lulled by the slow rocking of the balloon, Dorothy and Toto fell fast asleep.

2

Omby Amby Fires
a Shot

In a far-off place beyond clouds and rainbows, in the center of the Land of Oz, the beautiful young Princess Ozma slowly climbed the green marble staircase of the Emerald Palace with her friend and adviser, the Scarecrow. Ozma was quiet, and the kind Scarecrow sensed her discouragement.

"Perhaps today Dorothy will signal that she wishes to return to us, Your Majesty," he said.

"That is certainly my heart's desire," said

Ozma. "But I am not very hopeful anymore. Every Saturday for months we have faithfully watched for Dorothy's signal on the magic picture. But it never comes. She gives no sign of thinking of us. I am afraid she has forgotten all about us!"

"Cluck, cluck, ca-daw-cut," said Billina the Yellow Hen as Ozma and the Scarecrow entered Ozma's private room. "You are almost late! I was afraid you weren't coming! What would I do if Dorothy signaled? I have no wand! I can't work magic! I could not bring her here! Ca-daw-cut!"

"There, there," soothed Ozma. "Come and sit down. I'm sorry we made you worry."

Billina hopped into Ozma's lap, and the three friends watched the magic picture. Peaceful scenes from all over Oz showed on the magic screen. The Cowardly Lion walked serenely through the forest. The Tin Woodman played gently with some Winkie children. Suddenly the picture changed from Oz to Kansas. Now, instead of Oz, a small dusty farm could be seen—the home of Uncle Henry, Aunt Em, and

Dorothy. But where was Dorothy? She was not in her secret place in the hayloft. She was not in the barn doing chores. She was not in the barnyard feeding the chickens. She was not in the tire swing that hung from the old tree by the drive. She was not at the table with Aunt Em and Uncle Henry. She was not on her bed reading, either.

"How cozy Kansas looks," said Ozma. "Sometimes I would like to be an ordinary girl like Dorothy, living in a world where everything is exactly as it seems. Instead of taking care of others, I think I would like to be taken care of. Not for always—just for a little while."

The Scarecrow understood the young princess's yearning. Ozma was still quite young for the big job of ruling Oz.

"Perhaps one day, Your Majesty," he said. "But right now the question is *where is Dorothy?*"

Immediately the magic picture became a blur of colors and lines. Then suddenly everything came into focus again. There in the sky were Dorothy and Toto, swinging in the basket beneath the beautiful balloon. They were still sleeping. Far below them was the Dangerous Desert that surrounded the four lands of Oz and protected the land and the Emerald City at its center from invaders.

"Why, Dorothy is coming *here!*" Ozma exclaimed. "Oh, Scarecrow, isn't it wonderful? We must go at once to welcome her!"

The Scarecrow's face was serious. He was staring at the fire that heated the air in the balloon and kept it aloft. The fire grew smaller. It flickered and went out.

"We must go at once and *rescue* her!" said the Scarecrow. "For the balloon is falling out of the sky, and soon it will land in the Dangerous Desert. Then the balloon and Dorothy will be swallowed up by the enchanted sand!"

Immediately Ozma changed from wistful girl to royal ruler. She quickly summoned Omby Amby, captain of the armies of Oz and commander of the Royal Body Guard.

"Sound the alarm," Ozma ordered.

"What alarm, Your Majesty?" said Omby Amby. "There is no alarm in the palace."

"Then fire a shot!" she said.

"Fire a shot?" Omby Amby was horrified. Though he always carried a rifle, he had never before fired one and was quite reluctant to do so. But Omby Amby was above all an obedient soldier. So after pulling his enormous hat completely down over his head to protect his ears, he held his breath and fired his rifle into the air. The effect of the crack of the rifle in the still afternoon was astonishing, for never before in the history of Oz had a shot been fired. The people of the Emerald City poured into the streets and streamed toward the palace to see what the matter was.

From the palace balcony Ozma told the dreadful news.

"What can we do? How can we help?" called her subjects.

"Keep to your homes and hope for the best," said Ozma. "I am going to help Dorothy myself, and I am counting on you to keep peace in the Emerald City while I am away."

"Yes, of course. We will, Your Majesty," they responded.

Ozma sent Omby Amby to harness up the Sawhorse to her red wagon. Then she herself hastened to the talking head of the Gump, which hung in the palace hallway.

Once before, the Gump had been placed at the head of an important mission. Two sofas had been lashed together for his body. Wings and magic had been added to give him life as a satisfactory if cumbersome flying creature. But when the mission was over he had asked to be returned to his place on the palace wall. Ozma now asked him if he would allow himself to be reconstructed. At first he declined, for he had found his life as a flying contraption both hazardous and awkward. But when Ozma explained that he was needed to rescue Dorothy, he readily agreed, for like everyone else in Oz who knew her, he loved the little girl from Kansas.

Hastily reassembled, the Gump prepared for

takeoff from the palace roof, with Billina and the Scarecrow on board.

"Take care," said Ozma. "And may you find Dorothy in time."

Ozma hastened to the palace door, where the red wagon drawn by her faithful Sawhorse stood ready and waiting. Omby Amby helped her into the wagon and then climbed aboard himself with a large carpetbag.

"Just a few necessities," explained Omby Amby respectfully.

The Scarecrow and Billina peered over the edge of the Gump on the palace roof.

"Farewell, Your Majesty," they called.

"Farewell, dear friends," Ozma called back. "I shall meet you and Dorothy at the edge of the Dangerous Desert."

For a moment it appeared that the Gump's flight would be short indeed. He jumped off the roof, careened, swooped, and nearly collided with the palace spires. Then one of the palace banners draped itself over his eyes and Billina had to crawl out on his head to pull it off.

After that the Gump recovered his flying technique and headed directly toward the Dangerous Desert. Soon he and his crew were beyond the Emerald City, flying over the land of the Munchkins. The beauty of the land be-

low was breathtaking, but fear of what lay ahead made everyone nervous.

Not long after, they neared the desert. One minute all was rich and beautiful below—the next it was dry and stark and silent.

"We are now over the desert," Billina announced in a hushed voice.

Secret fear filled the hearts of the faithful three, for they knew that to land in the desert sand would be fatal. But thanks to her sharp bird's eyes it was not long before Billina sighted Dorothy's balloon drifting ahead.

"Hurry!" she cried from her post on the Gump's head. "The balloon is almost down!"

It was a tense and dangerous time, for now the Gump had two things to do at once that he had never been able to do separately. He had to hurry and he had to dive.

"We're going to crash!" shrieked Billina as they plummeted toward the desert.

"Hang on!" cried the Scarecrow.

There was one awful jolt as one of the Gump's sofa legs dug into the sand. This set the rest of the Gump and his passengers spinning around like a top.

"Help!" cried the Gump. "What shall I do?"

"I'm getting dizzy," said Billina. "What do you think?" she asked the Scarecrow.

"I'm thinking," he replied.

It was into this whirling confusion that the sleeping balloonists now landed. The jolt woke Dorothy and Toto, and when they opened their eyes they found, to their surprise, that the Scarecrow and Billina were sitting across from them in the Gump. There was no time for a

joyful reunion, because the spinning Gump was quickly boring into the sand of the Dangerous Desert and the imbedded sofa leg was disintegrating in the enchanted sand.

"Dorothy, quick!" called the Scarecrow. "Take some of my stuffing and build a fire. You, Gump, flap your wings. Flap as you have never flapped before!"

So the Gump flapped, and Dorothy kindled a fire with straw from the Scarecrow's legs. Slowly the balloon filled with hot air, and in a moment, sure enough, they were airborne again.

But the crisis was far from over. Unless more fuel could be found the fire would soon go out. Inspired by the Scarecrow, the Gump offered his remaining seven sofa legs for fuel. (They had never been brought to life and were therefore not of much use to him anyway.)

They managed cleverly and bravely for a time, but it was soon clear that they could never reach the edge of the desert. There was not nearly enough fuel, and now the loosely constructed Gump was starting to fall apart.

Again, it was Billina's turn to be brave. Like most hens she was not a good flier. She could, of course, jump and flap in such a way as to get to the top of a henhouse if there was a fox in the yard. But real flight was something she was not built for and had never attempted. Yet now she volunteered to fly to Ozma for help. With her head thrust forward as far as she could manage and her short legs tucked up under her round little tummy in as streamlined a fashion as possible, Billina took off.

Ozma waited anxiously at the edge of the desert, watching carefully for any sign of Dorothy and her rescuers. Suddenly, with a soft thud, a bird fell at her feet. Omby Amby stepped forward to remove the sorry dead creature, but Ozma stopped him.

"No! Wait!" she cried. "It's Billina!"

For several minutes the exhausted hen lay unconscious in Ozma's arms. At last her eyes fluttered open and she began to speak.

"Oh, if only I had my magic green carpet,"

said Ozma, sighing, after she heard Billina's report. "Then I would roll it out under Dorothy and go to save her. Why didn't we think to bring it?"

"I thought to bring it, Your Majesty," said Omby Amby.

"How wonderful!" said Ozma.

"But the royal housekeeper had sent it to the laundry," said Omby Amby.

"How awful!" said Ozma.

"So I went to the laundry to get it," said Omby Amby.

"How wonderful!" said Ozma.

"But the royal laundryman said I couldn't take it because it wasn't dry," said Omby Amby.

"How awful!" said Ozma.

"But I said, 'The princess has need of it,' " said Omby Amby. "And I took it anyway."

"How wonderful!" said Ozma.

"But it is still very damp, to say the least," said Omby Amby as he produced the dripping thing from his carpetbag.

"Never mind!" cried Ozma gratefully. "Unroll it at once!"

When they touched the carpet it was cool and wet. Indeed, although it was rolled up like a carpet, it actually seemed to be made of water and looked less green than blue. At Ozma's command the carpet unfurled itself and became a river of beautiful blue water that flowed straight out into the desert. Ozma climbed into the red wagon and ordered the Sawhorse and Billina to do the same. Then Omby Amby pushed it into the magic water, where it instantly became a boat with oars. Omby Amby pushed off and boarded the wagon boat, and the little crew headed out into the desert to meet Dorothy.

Dorothy and the Scarecrow had almost given up hope when suddenly the Gump let out a joyful cry.

"Water, ho!" he called.

Dorothy and the Scarecrow were amazed. There in the desert a ribbon of beautiful blue water was unfurling toward them. Steam rose from the front and sides of the magic carpet where the cool blue water touched the hot sand.

Ever so gently they splashed into the river. The balloon drifted away, and the passengers of the Gump found themselves adrift.

"I feel a little lightheaded," said the head of the Gump, whose sofa parts had sunk and who was now floating upside down, "and not entirely in my right mind—can't tell whether I'm coming or going," he continued as he began to drift away.

"I've got you," said Dorothy, grabbing on to one of his horns.

"Could you possibly give me a hand too?" asked the Scarecrow. "I seem to be in a bit of a—glub, glub."

With that the Scarecrow, whose pants legs were empty and heavily water-soaked, disappeared under water. He would have sunk entirely if Dorothy had not grabbed him by his pointed hat and held his head above water.

So it was that Dorothy saved everyone except Toto, who was capably dog-paddling about on his own. But now what was Dorothy to do? She could not swim to shore in the Dangerous Desert. Nor could she possibly swim to the edge of the desert. In fact, she was already very tired.

Just when Dorothy thought she could not continue any longer, she felt something hard touch her shoulder. She turned to see Omby Amby reaching out with an oar to help her into the red wagon boat. Never had Ozma, who was standing in the bow, looked quite so beautiful to Dorothy.

"Dorothy," she said with great affection, "I am so glad that you have come."

As soon as the travelers reached the edge of the Dangerous Desert they stopped to gather straw and restuff the Scarecrow's legs.

"Oh, thank you!" said the Scarecrow as he took a few steps on the bank. "It's good to stand on solid ground again. I never did quite get my sea legs."

"Of course not," said the Sawhorse drily. "You didn't have any legs at all!"

"With your permission, Your Majesty," said the Scarecrow, "we will go ahead to prepare a welcome. And if I may make a suggestion, why don't you and Dorothy continue on the magic blue carpet? I'm sure it will do you both good to be alone for a while."

"How wise and thoughtful you are," said Ozma.

So Omby Amby and the Scarecrow rode off toward the Emerald City on the Sawhorse, with the head of the Gump tied on behind, and Ozma, Dorothy, Billina, and Toto continued through the Land of Oz on the magic blue carpet.

3

An Intruder
in the Palace

Clump, clump, clump. The noise resounded through the palace halls. *Whoosh, whoosh, whoosh.* It whispered loudly from the palace stair. *Bounce, bounce,* "Wheee!" It ricocheted off the walls of the royal bedroom.

If Ozma had been there, she would have said firmly, "No running in the royal hallway. None whatsoever!"

If Omby Amby had been there, he would have said sternly, "No sliding on the royal bannister. And absolutely no bouncing on the royal bed!"

But Ozma was with Dorothy, floating on the magic blue carpet. And Omby Amby was halfway between the Dangerous Desert and the Emerald City. So nobody said anything to the intruder in the empty palace.

With a skip, a hop, and a jump, he skidded through the polished green marble halls and slid to a stop before an enormous jeweled mirror. He took one look at himself and stuck out his tongue. He watched, fascinated, as the reflection in the mirror stuck its tongue out at him. It was not the tongue of a villain or a monster. Rather, it belonged to a very small yellow-haired boy. Because he was so small, some called him Speck. Because he never walked when he could hop and never hopped when he could skip, some called him Skip. Because he always had a bright red circle on each cheek from all his hopping and skipping, some called him Patch.

"But my real name," said Speck-Skip-Patch

to himself, "is Robert. And I am the king of this castle."

He drew himself up and strutted off down the hall.

"Speck!" came a voice from outside the palace. "Where are you?"

The boy jumped. It was his mother!

"Skip! Patch! Where are you?" came the voices of his father and sisters and brothers.

There was a knocking at the palace door. The boy heard a servant downstairs going to answer. Now his heart beat faster, for he knew very well he should not be alone in the royal palace. Robert knew all about the palace, for his parents were the royal gardeners, and he came here every day with them to bring fresh flowers. He had been doing it from the time he was a tot, clinging to his mother's skirts. And as he grew he, too, brought the princess's flowers—green lilacs for the throne room, green and white roses for the royal bedroom, green lilies for the stair. Only this morning he had arranged a bouquet for the palace mantelpiece himself. He had even seen Ozma use her magic wand. How often when he worked in the palace garden had Robert wished for a wand like that! A wand could do the weeding in no time. A wand could water flowerbeds in a minute. A wand could remove the thorns that pricked a boy when he was sent to pick roses. But only Ozma had a magic wand.

Robert knew his way around the palace, but now, hearing footsteps on the stair, he panicked. After quickly removing his shoes, he turned and ran down a long corridor, which ended at the huge double doors of the throne room.

"Patch! Are you up here?" came a voice from the top of the stair.

The boy sucked in his breath and slipped into the throne room, closing the big doors behind him.

Voices of family and palace servants came and went in the corridor. Heads poked in at the door, but nobody noticed the little stocking feet showing beneath the throne room curtains.

"Patch! Speck! Skip!" they called, but Robert didn't answer.

He wanted to say, "Here I am!" and to leave his hiding place. But it was such a bad thing to have entered the throne room without the princess's permission that he was afraid to speak up.

"As soon as the coast is clear," he whispered to himself, "I'll tiptoe down the stairs, creep out through the window, and go straight home. 'Oh, what a nice walk I had in the woods,' I'll say. 'Oh,' they'll answer. 'Is that where you were? We were looking all over for you.' "

The voices came and went. Then they were gone. At last Robert ventured from behind the curtains. He thought he would go home at once, but first he could not resist climbing up on Ozma's throne. He placed his stocking feet upon the royal footstool and waved an imaginary wand in the air, just as he had seen Ozma wave her real one.

"I think I'll order up some ice cream," he said, waving the pretend wand. "Oh, now it's raining. I think I'll order up a rainbow—yes, please, right over there." He waved the imaginary wand at his feet. "Tie my shoes. Make the bed. Pull up the weeds."

He sighed. How wonderful it would be to have a real magic wand!

Robert turned over on his stomach, climbed down off the throne, and went toward the door. He really meant to leave at once, but then by the door, on an elegant table, Robert noticed a slender case. It was long and black with golden hinges and a jeweled lock, and it rested on a beautifully woven green cloth embroidered with the colorful symbols of each of the four lands of Oz. What could be inside?

Robert's curiosity got the better of him. He opened the jeweled latches and raised the lid, and a bright green light sparkled up from the case. Robert gasped. On the green satin lining, as delicate and beautiful as Ozma herself, was Ozma's wonderful wand!

Robert quickly closed the case and started again toward the door. Then he turned and went back. Once again he carefully opened the case that held the wand. He lifted it slowly, admiring the jeweled star at the top. Then he walked thoughtfully back across the throne room, waving the wand in the air.

"I'll just try it," he said. "Just once. Now, what will it be? Hmmm. Perhaps I'll order a candy cane. Or a toy train. Or a giant red lollipop."

He climbed onto the throne to make up his mind.

Billina's Narrow Escape

All this time Dorothy and Ozma were rowing along in the wagon boat on the magic blue carpet. Billina lay happily in Ozma's lap, listening to Dorothy's stories about Kansas.

"Humph," she said when she heard of the yellow hen at the fair. "No upbringing. No manners. A disgrace to henhood!"

Toto stood on the bow of the wagon boat, looking ahead. Suddenly he began to bark excitedly and then hopped into the boat to jump up at Dorothy. He barked at her, then returned to the bow and barked at the water.

Dorothy and Ozma looked to see what could be upsetting him so. Hundreds of silver lights flashed upon the surface of the water, followed by hundreds of tiny splashes. School upon school of tiny silver fish came leaping along the surface of the magic blue carpet. At the sight of them Billina, too, hopped up on the edge of the wagon boat.

"Delicious fishes!" she said. She leaned over

to snatch a fish from the stream and fell—*ker-plop!*—into the water. She flapped her wings wildly, splashed desperately, and sank like a stone.

"Billina!" Dorothy cried. "Ozma, save her!"

For the very first time since setting out from the palace, Ozma had need of her magic wand. With the wand she could have turned Billina into a chicken fish or given her webbed feet for swimming or made the river run dry. Without it her usual royal calm left her.

"My wand!" she said helplessly. "I forgot to bring it! Dorothy, I don't know what to do!"

Without her wand Ozma was helpless. And Billina was drowning! To Dorothy it seemed impossible for such an awful thing to happen in the magical land of Oz. Then Madame Zsa Zsa's words came back to her. "There is a time for magic and a time for common sense." Suddenly she knew what to do. Down she dived, just as she had done a thousand times in the swimming hole back home. She swam straight to the bottom, grabbed Billina, and pushed back up to the surface. She handed the wet hen to Ozma and then climbed back into the boat.

"Hold her upside down," said Dorothy, "to let the water come out." Ozma obeyed. In a moment Billina made a little sound halfway between a cluck and a cough, and began to breathe again.

"Dorothy!" said Ozma. "How did you do that?"

"Do what?" said Dorothy.

"How did you stay alive under the water

without air? What charm did you use?"

Dorothy realized that Ozma did not know how to swim.

"No charm," she said. "I just swam." She explained what swimming was and promised to teach Ozma how to do it before returning to Kansas.

After that they saw many more fish—much bigger ones. Hundreds upon thousands came rushing down the river. Because it was an enchanted river, the fish in it were enchanted as well. Some of the bigger ones could speak.

"Turn back!" they warned. "There is danger ahead!"

Hordes of fish fled down the magic blue river, but Dorothy and Ozma kept on. As they drew closer to the city the sky grew dark with thunderclouds. But these clouds were green! Then they heard a great rumbling. This was followed by the sound of footsteps and the sight of crowds of Ozma's loyal subjects running *away* from the Emerald City!

The royal cook ran by and, seeing Ozma, called out, "Oh, Princess, turn back! Flee while you can, for there is something terrible in the Emerald City!"

"What is it?" asked Ozma. "What is happening?"

But the royal cook was gone.

When Dorothy and Ozma reached the Emerald City at last, the gatekeeper was not there to let them in.

"Hello," called Dorothy.

"Open the gates," called Ozma.

There was only silence for a moment. Then the bushes nearby parted and two heads poked out. One was the Scarecrow's. The other was Omby Amby's. They both looked frightened.

"Thank goodness you have come," said the Scarecrow. "We are the only ones left in the city—"

Suddenly there was a great rumbling sound. It sounded like thunder, but it was lower and louder. Dorothy and Ozma put out their hands to feel the rain.

"No," said the Scarecrow. "It is not the weather. And it is not coming from the sky. That rumbling sound is from the palace. It's been like this all afternoon. At one o'clock," he explained, "green smoke poured from the palace windows. That's what made the green clouds. Right after that, huge hailstones fell all over the city, and everyone fled. Since then there has been nothing but this frightful noise. It never lasts long, and it only comes once in a while. But it shakes the palace and has caused a great deal of damage."

"It's an enchantment," said Ozma. "We must go to the palace at once to get my wand. Magic must be fought with magic."

As they approached the palace the rumbling came again. This time it was so loud that it

57

shook the palace walls. Jewels fell from the trim, and green glass shattered and dropped from the windows.

"Look out!" cried the Scarecrow as some of the glass fell into the water.

"It is too dangerous to enter by the door," he said. "We could be killed by falling glass if the great sound comes again."

"Besides," said Omby Amby timidly, "shouldn't we try to sneak up on the enemy without being seen?"

"Let's take the underground tunnel," said Ozma. "It was dug by King Roquat and his men."

At her command the magic blue carpet circled the palace and flowed into King Roquat's tunnel, where it wound beneath the palace through many underground rooms. The tunnel was dark and cool, and the voyagers kept silent, but even the smallest sounds and tiniest lappings of water echoed loudly in the cold, stony passageways.

"Woof!" Toto barked.

"Woowoowoowoowoowoowoof!" came the echo.

"Quiet, Toto," whispered Dorothy. "We don't know who is here or where he may be hiding."

"Or th-th-th-they!" said Omby Amby.

"Or *it*!" said the Scarecrow.

BAROOM! BARUMBLE!

The strange sound came again, even more loudly this time. Dorothy and Ozma held hands. Omby Amby jumped into the Scarecrow's arms. Billina flapped onto the Scarecrow's head.

"I can't see, Billina," complained the Scarecrow. "Your wing is over my face."

"Shh!" said Dorothy. "Listen! The noise is coming from above. Where are the stairs?"

Ozma pointed the way and the brave friends left the wagon boat. They followed Ozma up a narrow stairway and tiptoed into the palace hall, where fragments of green from the shattered chandelier sparkled on the marble floor. Before Dorothy could stop him, Toto took off down the hallway, searching for the source of the noise. But soon he returned. Whoever or whatever it was, it was not hiding on the first floor of the palace.

The friends climbed up the big winding palace staircase and Toto bounded away.

"W-wait! Come back, Toto!" whispered Dorothy. "Don't go so far ahead."

The little dog stopped at the top of the stairs and twitched his ears. He sniffed to the right. He sniffed to the left. Then he sped straight down the long corridor to the throne room and began to scratch at the door. Dorothy and the others ran after him.

"Toto! Stop! No! Don't go in there!" cried Dorothy.

But even if Toto had listened to Dorothy, he could not have obeyed her. For as little and light as he was, the moment he leaned on the heavy doors they swung open and Toto tumbled into the throne room. Dorothy and her friends skidded to a stop, piling up on one another in the doorway behind him.

Except for a small "Awk!" from Billina and a quiet gasp from everyone else, there was nothing but stunned silence—even Toto was still. Before the astonished group, filling up almost the entire throne room, was a gigantic green creature.

5

Ozma Casts a Spell

Everyone was so amazed at the sight that for a moment no one spoke (or clucked or barked).

The creature was bald and bumpy, and so huge that his head nearly touched the ceiling. His eyes sat right on top of his head, and perhaps because his head was so high or because of the way his eyes were set, he seemed completely unaware of the small astonished visitors at his feet.

63

"The wand," whispered Dorothy to the Scarecrow. "Where is it?"

Keeping his eyes glued on the huge green creature, the Scarecrow reached through the doorway and felt for the wand case.

"I have it!" he whispered, then withdrew the case and presented it to Ozma. But when Ozma opened the case, she found it empty!

The group stood there wondering what to do. Then in the silence they heard a sniffle— just one—from across the room. Past the giant creature was Ozma's throne, and emerging from behind it was a pair of small stockinged feet.

"Who's there?" demanded the Scarecrow. "We see you, so speak up at once."

The sniffle became a whimper, the whimper became a sob, the sob turned into a wail, and a little yellow head peeked out from behind the throne.

"I-I didn't mean it!" cried Robert. "I didn't know this would happen. I only meant to try it. But it didn't work right. It wouldn't do what I said!"

"What didn't work?" asked Dorothy.

Between sobs Robert tried to explain what had happened. He told of how he had dreamed of having a wand—to weed the garden and take the thorns from roses. He described how he had found Ozma's wand and tried to do things with it, but how nothing he tried had turned out right.

"I only wanted to make a rainbow," he said. "But all I got was some awful green smoke. Then I asked for wind to make the smoke go away, and all I got was a horrible hailstorm! After that I was hungry, so I wished for a big red lollipop. But instead when I waved the wand I got—him!" he wailed, pointing at the giant green creature. "And he keeps making this frightful noise! I am so afraid when he makes it! Oh, what's going to happen to me? I'm so sorry! And I'm so *scared*!" The little boy started sobbing.

"Where is the wand?" asked the Scarecrow.

"There," said Robert, pointing to the floor in front of the throne. "When the monster came I dropped it and hid back here. I can't reach it, and I don't dare come out."

The three friends in the doorway looked at each other. The wand was lying on the far side of the room, right by the huge green monster's foot. How could they recover it?

All this time the creature continued to sit there and stare at the ceiling. In fact, he had done nothing but sit there all afternoon, ever since Robert had conjured him up with Ozma's wand. There was very little room for him to move, and it seemed to be his nature not to move around very much anyway. But now, having sat still for such a long time, the creature began to move. He pushed off a little with his two huge hind feet and attempted to turn around.

Up until now Toto had been sitting, ears up, turning his head this way and that and watching the conversation between his friends in the doorway and the yellow-haired boy. But when the big creature tried to turn around, the room shook, and that was too much for Toto. He

charged, barking loudly and snapping excitedly at the creature's big green feet.

In fact, this was the first time that the big green creature was aware that there was anyone else in the room with him. For the first time he lowered himself and looked about the floor of the throne room. When he did this he noticed two things. The first was a little black speck of a creature darting back and forth in front of him. The second was that he was hungry. At once there issued from his mouth a long unrolling thing. It was the creature's tongue and it unfurled very quickly at Toto and then rolled back up. Fortunately Toto jumped away just in time to avoid being eaten.

"Chugarum," said the disappointed creature. "Chugarum. CHUGARUM!"

It was only a small expression of dissatisfaction, but because the creature was so huge it sounded like a tremendous roar. The whole palace shook, and the tinkling sound of falling glass was heard outside.

For once the fearless Toto was terrified. Yelping and whining, he ran to Dorothy and hid behind her.

"Why, that's nothing but a big old bullfrog!" cried Dorothy. "Just a big dumb old bullfrog! We have lots of them back home, only they're not so big. You big bully!" she said angrily. "How dare you try to hurt poor Toto! You ought to be ashamed of yourself—a great big thing like you picking on such a sweet little dog! Don't you know how to behave? In Kansas all the frogs are musicians. They sit on lily pads and sing. Everybody loves them. They don't go around scaring everybody and breaking things! You should just be ashamed of yourself for all the trouble you've caused."

"How was I to know it was a dog?" grumbled the frog when he could get a word in edge-wise. "I thought it was a bug. And it's not my fault that I'm here," he added morosely. "I don't even know how I came. I don't like this place one bit. I can't turn around, I'm hungry, I'm dry, and I'm uncomfortable. I'd much rather be back in my pond."

"There, there, of course you would," said Dorothy kindly. "I'm sorry for getting so angry. And if you'd like to be a normal-sized frog, I'm sure Ozma can help you."

"Oh, yes, thank you!" said the giant frog politely.

"Very well, then," said Dorothy. She walked over and picked up Ozma's magic wand.

Everyone, especially Robert, watched in awe as Ozma raised her wand.

"It's all in the chanting," she said to Robert. "You have to know the magic words." Then she waved the wand, singing softly:

> "Chugarum and chugarilly,
> Riverbank and water lily."

Very lightly Ozma touched the gigantic bullfrog on the shoulder. Instantly he disappeared.

"Where did he go, Your Majesty?" Robert asked.

"I sent him to a magic blue river where he will be much happier," she said. "And now I think I shall send you home to bed where you will be much happier also."

The boy's parents were sent for. At first they were quite angry with Robert, but Ozma calmed them gently.

"Robert has indeed been very naughty," she said. "But I believe he has suffered quite enough."

She took the boy on her lap.

"There are many kinds of magic in the world," she said. "Here in the Emerald City only a princess may have a magic wand for fixing things and keeping order. But," she added, "there is always magic in a good idea. And your idea that roses don't need thorns is such a good idea. Therefore I would like to appoint you the royal dethorner."

Ozma waved her wand, whispered a chant, and a small blue case appeared in Robert's hand. He opened it at once. Inside was a small silver wand, shaped like a delicate thornless rose.

"Whenever you touch a rose with this wand," said Ozma, "its thorns will disappear."

The boy hugged Ozma, and he and his parents went home. For a while after that, Ozma used her wand to clean the Emerald City and repair the palace. She finished as night fell. Then, after sending Omby Amby out to inform

her subjects that they could return safely to their homes, she sat down with her friends in the now-peaceful throne room.

From the magic blue carpet far below came a lovely, soothing song:

> "Chugarum and chugarilly,
> Riverbank and water lily."

It was the bullfrog, singing a lullaby for the Emerald City.

6

The Return of Madame Zsa Zsa

Morning came and Dorothy looked out the palace window. The big round orange sun was rising. And there on the horizon was a much smaller round ball—a blue and orange one. Even though it was still far away, Dorothy saw that it was a balloon just like the one that had brought her to Oz. It was floating straight toward the Emerald City, and Dorothy felt sure, somehow, that it was coming to take her home.

She and Ozma and Toto went outside. They

walked beside the magic blue carpet that lay drying on the lawn in the morning sun. As it dried and became a true carpet again, a beautiful pattern appeared on it. The border was of golden fishes, and woven into the center was a beautiful silver frog surrounded by water lilies. The royal groundskeepers prepared to roll it up.

"When will the frog sing in Oz again?" Dorothy asked.

"When you return to Oz," said Ozma. "Then we will unroll the magic carpet so you can teach me to swim, and the frog will sing."

The balloon drew closer. Dorothy and Ozma climbed a hill to meet it and were surprised to see that there was someone in the passenger basket—a gypsy fortune teller holding a crystal ball. One of her eyes had a distinctly kind look. The other was decidedly stern.

"Why, it's Madame Zsa Zsa!" Dorothy exclaimed. "She was at the fair in Kansas. I met her just before I left. I'm almost sure she had something to do with my coming back to Oz."

"What are you doing here?" asked Ozma when they reached the fortune teller. "Are you from Kansas or from Oz?"

"Both," said Madame Zsa Zsa.

"Is that a crystal ball or a fishbowl?" asked Dorothy.

"Both," said Madame Zsa Zsa.

"Are you real or magic?" Ozma asked.

"Both," said Madame Zsa Zsa.

Ozma and Dorothy looked at each other and then at Madame Zsa Zsa.

"Who are you *really*?" they asked.

Immediately Madame Zsa Zsa disappeared and in her place stood two beautiful women. One was pale, with flowing red curls and a magic wand. She was dressed in a lacy white gown, and the look in her eyes was sweet and kind. The other was tan and strong, and wore her dark hair in braids around her head. She was dressed in a simple cotton gown, and the look in her eyes, though not at all unkind, was matter-of-fact and reassuring. Dorothy and Ozma recognized the first woman as Glinda the

Good, the witch of the South, who had helped them many times before.

"Glinda!" cried Ozma joyfully. "What are you doing here?"

"I am your fairy godmother," Glinda revealed. "I will always be here when you need me. And this is Glenda," she said, indicating the other woman. "She is Dorothy's fairy godmother in Kansas."

"But there's no magic in Kansas!" said Dorothy.

"Nonsense!" said Glenda. "As sure as there are frogs in Oz, there is magic in Kansas. You just have to look for it."

The two fairy godmothers spoke together. "There is a time for magic and a time for common sense. It is important to know which is which."

"And," Glinda continued, "it is important to have a little of both. Back in Kansas you, Dorothy, were forgetting the magical side of life. And here in Oz you, Ozma, were depending too much on magic and forgetting the importance of common sense. So we, your fairy godmothers, joined together to bring you and your two worlds together again."

"But now it is time for Dorothy to return home for a while," said Glenda.

"This time," said Ozma, "please don't stay away so long."

"I won't," said Dorothy. "You can be sure of that. I will come back soon—I promise."

Dorothy thanked the two fairy godmothers and said good-bye to Ozma. Then she and Toto climbed into the passenger basket. This time there was no rope to untie, no sandbags to release. As soon as Toto and Dorothy were aboard, the balloon took off.

It had been raining in Kansas. So for the first time in a long while it was cool enough for Dorothy to play in the barn loft. There in an old chest she found Uncle Henry's old soldier clothes and a beautiful carved ivory fan. In the bottom of the chest she came upon an envelope that she had never noticed before. It was filled with old documents—a school diploma, a marriage license, the last will and testament of an old great-uncle she had never known, and Aunt Em's birth certificate. "Born to Hiram and Gladys Todd in Plainville, Kansas," it read. "A baby girl. Weight: 6 pounds 5 ounces. Name: Emily Glenda."

"Emily *Glenda*!" Dorothy exclaimed to herself. "Oh, Aunt Em!"

Just then Aunt Em's head poked up through the trap door.

"Come along now, Dorothy. Storm's coming up again. Got to bring in the wash."